First published in Great Britain in 2014 by Boxer® Books Limited.

www.boxerbooks.com

Boxer ® is a registered trademark of Boxer Books Limited.

Based on an original idea by Sam Williams.

Monstrous Stories™ concept, names, stories, designs and logos
© Boxer Books Limited

Written by Paul Harrison
Paul Harrison asserts his moral right to be identified
as the author of this work.
Text copyright © 2014 Boxer Books Limited

Illustrated by Tom Knight
Tom Knight asserts his moral right to be identified
as the illustrator of this work.
Illustrations copyright © 2014 Tom Knight

The illustrations were prepared using brush, ink and digital.
The text is set in Blackmoor Plain and Adobe Caslon.

ISBN 978-1-907967-79-5
1 3 5 7 9 10 8 6 4 2

Printed in Great Britain

All of our papers are sourced from
managed forests and renewable resources.

Dr Roach's
Monstrous STORIES

r Roach presents

RACCOON OF
DOOM

a Boxer® Books production

Contents

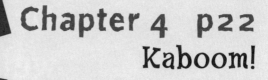

Dr Roach welcomes YOU!

Have you ever smelled a raccoon's gigantic bottom burp? Not for the squeamish, I can tell you. Raccoons can be rather cute really - unless they have been eating the wrong food.

One night, our greedy friend finds some rather tasty morsels that turn him into a crazy monster with laser-beam eyes set on destroying the town of Hummerfield in search of more food!

Luckily for the townsfolk, young Jimmy Schwartz is on the trail of the raccoon of doom and saves the day.

How, you ask? Come closer, my friend, and I'll tell you all about it.

Welcome to Dr Roach's Monstrous Stories. Enjoy!

Dr Roach

Chapter 1
Cold, Wet and Hungry

Jimmy Schwartz was bored. The rain had been falling all day long so he had been stuck indoors. His house was in the middle of the woods; there were lots of trees, not many people and little to do on a day like this. Jimmy had been staring out of the window for more than an hour.

"Yes! There it is," shouted Jimmy. "Mum, can I feed the raccoon?"

"Oh not that thing again!" his mother replied.

"Please," whined Jimmy.

"OK, give it an apple. But don't be long: supper's ready and I don't want you getting soaked."

Jimmy's mum was probably the worst cook in the world. Jimmy would rather have had the apple and given his supper to the raccoon. Nevertheless Jimmy dashed outside with the fruit, tossed it to the raccoon and ran back inside to watch from the window. The raccoon stared at the food in disgust. 'Fruit?! Fruit?!' thought the raccoon. 'If I wanted to eat that sort of nonsense, I'd go back to the woods!'

But the raccoon could smell Jimmy's supper. Jimmy might not have liked his mother's food, but the raccoon had fairly low standards. At least it made a change from berries and worms. He followed Jimmy to the house but by now the door was closed. The raccoon was cold, wet and hungry. What was he going to do?

Then he smelt something new.
It was faint but it was definitely
FOOD! The raccoon gave himself a
shake and headed hungrily towards it.

Jimmy watched the raccoon as
it waddled off, leaving the apple
uneaten on the ground.

"Now where are you going?"
he wondered.

Chapter 2
Paradise

Hummerfield was paradise for a hungry raccoon. It was full of places to eat and they all looked magnificent! The lights from the burger bars, pizza restaurants and chicken joints shimmered on the damp pavements. The enticing smells from the café teased the raccoon's nose and the sounds of food being eaten were like music to its ears. The raccoon tried the nearest restaurant. No sooner had it got in the door than the trouble started.

In went the raccoon.

"SHRIEK!" went the customers.

"THWACK!" went the waiter with a tray.

And out went the raccoon, flat on its bottom on the wet pavement.

This was going to be harder than the raccoon had imagined. The same thing happened everywhere. In,

13

shriek, thwack, out. At the last café
the raccoon was pushed out with a
broom and landed with a SPLASH in
a large puddle on the pavement.

The raccoon sat in the puddle and
felt hungry and hopeless, but mainly
hungry. The raccoon could still smell
food. This time it was very, very
close. He looked about and there
right behind him was a rubbish bin.

The smell was coming from inside.
The raccoon could climb on top of the
bin with ease, but there was a problem
– some kind of lid. With a bit of
fiddling the raccoon found it could
push the lid off. Once inside, he found

what he was looking for – a half-eaten
pizza. Admittedly it was slightly stale
and a little bit mouldy, but that didn't
bother the raccoon. A stale pizza still
tasted better than berries and worms.
He could eat at last!

Chapter 3
Food, Glorious Food

Once the raccoon had finished he realised that there were rubbish bins full of garbage all over town. But that was where the raccoon's good fortune ended. No matter how many bins he found none of them contained anything to eat. Were there no rubbish bins left in Hummerfield that had any food in them?

Actually yes, yes there was.

Not far from where the raccoon was slumped in despair a large rubbish bin was sitting open and its tempting aromas drifted across Hummerfield. The raccoon got the scent of it. The smell spoke of available treats, of half-eaten burger and fries! The raccoon was up like a shot and off on the trail of the tantalising smell with Jimmy Schwartz following close behind.

After much pleading with his mum, Jimmy had been on the raccoon's tail since it had so rudely turned its back on the apple Jimmy had left for it. The raccoon had no idea he was being followed. He only had eyes, ears and nose for food!

"So where are you off to now?" wondered Jimmy, his sense of smell not being as strong as the raccoon's.

He watched the raccoon scamper through an open set of gates and straight for a large rubbish bin. With an athletic leap that was surprising for such a tubby animal it was up and in.

The raccoon didn't know – or care
– where he was, but Jimmy knew.
The raccoon was in the rubbish bins
round the back of McScavengers,
the biggest burger restaurant in
Hummerfield. And the raccoon was
helping himself to all the leftover
food that was inside.

'Food, glorious food,' thought the
raccoon, grinning to himself.

Chapter 4
Kaboom!

Unfortunately for the raccoon there were all sorts of weird flavours, colourings and spices in the drinks, shakes, ketchups and sauces that he found in that rubbish bin, not to mention a million additives and preservatives from the new Megaburger. The raccoon slurped it all down – all the burgers, dippers and fries he could stuff in his fat face. The only thing he didn't eat was the gherkin from the burger – but then no one eats that.

When all that food hit the raccoon's stomach there was an awful gurgling noise. Everything he had eaten went swirling round and round in his gut.

The raccoon gave a shudder and there was a crackle of electricity around his body. Then his fur began to change colour. The raccoon's eyes nearly popped out of his head.

"It's been in there a very long time," Jimmy muttered to himself. "I wonder what it's doing?"

Curiosity overcame Jimmy's caution and he edged towards the massive rubbish bin.

25

Inside things were getting more
bizarre. Steam hissed out of the
raccoon's ears like a kettle
and its eyes began to
change colour
from yellow
to green to blue to
orange. The raccoon
was feeling really
weird now

and strangely powerful. It was also angry. Very angry.

Jimmy crept closer to the rubbish bin – he was nearly there when there was a big

KABOOM

and a bright rainbow flash of colour exploded upwards. Jimmy fell backwards and landed on his backside.

"What was that?" he cried.

Chapter 5
Help Needed!

Jimmy slowly got back to his feet.

"I hope the raccoon's OK," he said.

Two sets of claws clasped the top of the rubbish bin and the raccoon dragged himself out. It looked completely different from the

cuddly raccoon Jimmy had made friends with – it looked EVIL! It had glowing red eyes and the tips of its fur crackled and spat with sparks. The raccoon threw his head back and let out an enormous roar!

"I think I'm going to need some help!" said Jimmy, clambering to his feet and dashing off.

Whatever had happened inside that rubbish bin had made the raccoon starving hungry. His hunger needed sorting – and sorting immediately.

The raccoon followed
his nose and headed straight for the
front of McScavengers! The raccoon
didn't bother with trying to squirm
through the front door – instead the
furious fur ball simply fired two laser
beams from his eyes, melted the large
windows and stomped right in.

The raccoon went into a feeding frenzy. To a background of screams from the fleeing public the raccoon binged on everything McScavengers had to offer.

BUT HE
WAS STILL
HUNGRY!
So the
raccoon headed
downtown.

Chapter 6
Emergency Meeting

The police station was packed with people. At one end of the large entrance hall was the mayor, the chief of police, a wildlife expert, the manager of McScavengers and Jimmy.

"Please ladies and gentlemen," said the Chief Inspector, "we understand that you are all worried by the threat the raccoon is posing to our town."

"Arrest it!" someone shouted.

"It's unlikely our police cells would be able to hold it," replied the Chief. "First I think we need to establish what happened. Jimmy, you say you know this raccoon?"

"Yes sir, I used to feed it," Jimmy replied.

"It's his fault – arrest him!" the same person shouted.

"Order! Order!" shouted the mayor.

"It was really friendly," Jimmy continued.

"So why is it so grumpy now?" asked the mayor.

"That will be its diet," said the wildlife expert. "The fats and spices it's been eating have given it indigestion and made it grumpy. Not to mention the strange chemical reaction that has happened, as a result of mixing all the additives, preservatives and colourings, which explains its new powers!"

"It happened when it ate from the bin at McScavengers," said Jimmy.

"It's their fault, arrest them!" shouted the person in the audience.

"Chief Inspector, will you please arrest that man and put him somewhere we can't hear him," muttered the mayor.

"So what was in the bin?" the mayor asked.

"Old food: Megaburgers, Space Shakes, Fizz Slurps, Fire-breather Fries, just our normal menu," said the McScavengers manager.

"Hmm, well it certainly seems to have had a profound effect on the raccoon," said the wildlife expert.

"We've got to hope that as the results happened so quickly they'll fade away just as fast. The worst thing that could happen is that it eats any more spicy food; that would seem to increase its power."

"Well it's clear what we have to do – keep the raccoon away from spicy food and we should be OK," said the mayor.

40

The doors of the police station burst open and a police officer dashed in.

"The raccoon!" he shouted. "It's heading for the Grand Hotel!"

"Oh no!" cried the mayor. "That's where the Curry Festival is being held. It's a disaster!"

Chapter 7
The Raccoon of Doom

People ran screaming from the building and then ran screaming back in as coming towards them was …

"The raccoon of doom!" shouted a woman.

The raccoon was coming and it looked MEAN! Suddenly it stopped and sniffed hungrily at the air.

Somewhere nearby was food – and lots of it. Fortunately the raccoon couldn't read or it would have seen the big sign hanging from the Grand Hotel:

THE HUMMERFIELD CURRY FESTIVAL

Featuring the World's biggest curry!

"If the raccoon gets anywhere near that curry it will be the end of Hummerfield!" cried the mayor.

The good news was that the raccoon couldn't tell exactly where the delicious smells were coming from. The bad news was it had a good idea how to try and find them. It flashed its laser eyes at the buildings round about. One by one the windows, blinds and curtains melted away revealing in turn: office desks, a man in the tub with a rubber duck, a woman sound asleep in her bed with fluffy ear muffs on, two burglars about to rob a safe, and – particularly embarrassing – a boy sitting on the toilet reading a comic.

"We must stop that raccoon," shouted the Chief Inspector.

"Not just yet," shouted Mr Glaze, the local glass supplier.

"Oh do be quiet!" snapped the mayor.

"I calculate that its powers will disappear in five minutes if we can somehow neutralise its stomach acids," said the wildlife expert tapping away on his tablet computer.

"But how?" asked the mayor.

Before anyone could answer the laser beams from the crazy animal fell upon the Grand Hotel. The windows

melted away and the glorious smell
of the world's biggest curry billowed
out. The raccoon shuddered with
delight and a long string of saliva
drooled down from its mouth.

"Oh no!" cried the Chief Inspector.
"What now?"

Chapter 8
Too Much Gas!

Despite everything that was going on, when Jimmy smelled the wonderful aromas wafting from the hotel he couldn't help think about how good it was compared to the more 'cabbagey' stench that usually seeped from his mother's food. How she managed to make food that was burnt and soggy at the same time was truly unbelievable. In fact his stomach ached just thinking about it.

"That's it!" cried Jimmy.

"That's what?" asked the Chief Inspector.

"How about an indigestion tablet?" said Jimmy.

"Genius!" said the wildlife expert. "A settled stomach should make it calmer. But where do we get one?"

"Here," said the mayor scrabbling in her handbag. "I've always got some – it doesn't do to have gas at an official function. But how will we get the raccoon to eat it?"

"Don't worry, I'll deal with that," said Jimmy.

He grabbed the tablet and bravely ran outside. Everyone gasped – what was he doing? Jimmy held the tablet out to the raccoon.

Something seemed
to stir in the
deepest recesses
of the raccoon's
memory; it seemed
to remember that
Jimmy was its

friend. It sniffed
the tablet,
grabbed it in its
greedy paws and
wolfed it down.

There was
a dreadful
rumbling
sound from
the raccoon's
belly,

then gurgling
and then …

Nothing.

The raccoon
looked a bit
more content

with life. The angry laser eyes were
nearly back to normal. The fur didn't
crackle with electricity.

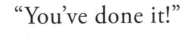

"You've done it!"
cried the mayor.

"I'm not so sure,"
said Jimmy. "It still
doesn't look quite
right to me."

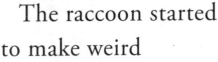

The raccoon started
to make weird

jerking movements,
like it was dancing
the robot. Its eyes
started to flash

different colours
and its tongue
popped in
and out of its
mouth.

"What's going
on?" said the
Chief Inspector.

The raccoon was now waggling its bottom in the air.

"Jimmy was right!" said the wildlife expert. "By my calculations too much gas has built up by the raccoon's chronic, chemically induced indigestion."

"What does that mean?" asked the mayor.

CRITICAL!

"It means the raccoon is about to blow!" said Jimmy.

The raccoon went stiff, clenched its eyes tight shut, dug its claws into the ground and

PPPAAAAAAR

a gigantic bottom burp exploded
from the raccoon's backside. Multi-
coloured rays shot out of its bum like
it was some furry, windy rainbow-
machine. Its eyes flickered and it
span round like a

RRRRRRPPPPP!!!!

trumping carousel. And the smell! The pungent pong of partially digested junk food settled over Hummerfield like rotting vegetables, causing everyone to gag and cough.

The raccoon flopped on its backside and sat there, looking confused but relieved. What it needed now was a bit of fruit, or perhaps some nuts. Up it hopped and trotted happily back off to the woods to look for its usual food.

"You know," thought Jimmy, tears streaming down his face from the rotten stench, "I don't think I'll complain about the smell of Mum's cooking ever again!"

Have you ever had a pet? Jenny has several – she loves roaches. And I agree. We are quite lovable! Unfortunately, her dad doesn't think so. He can't wait to exterminate all of us.

One night, some very irresponsible aliens dump their food waste on earth – with disastrous consequences. Imagine – people actually begin to turn into giant grapes. That's right – giant grapes!

How lucky then that Jenny's extraordinary pet roaches are here to save the world!

How, you ask? Get a copy today and I'll tell you everything!

Catch you later!

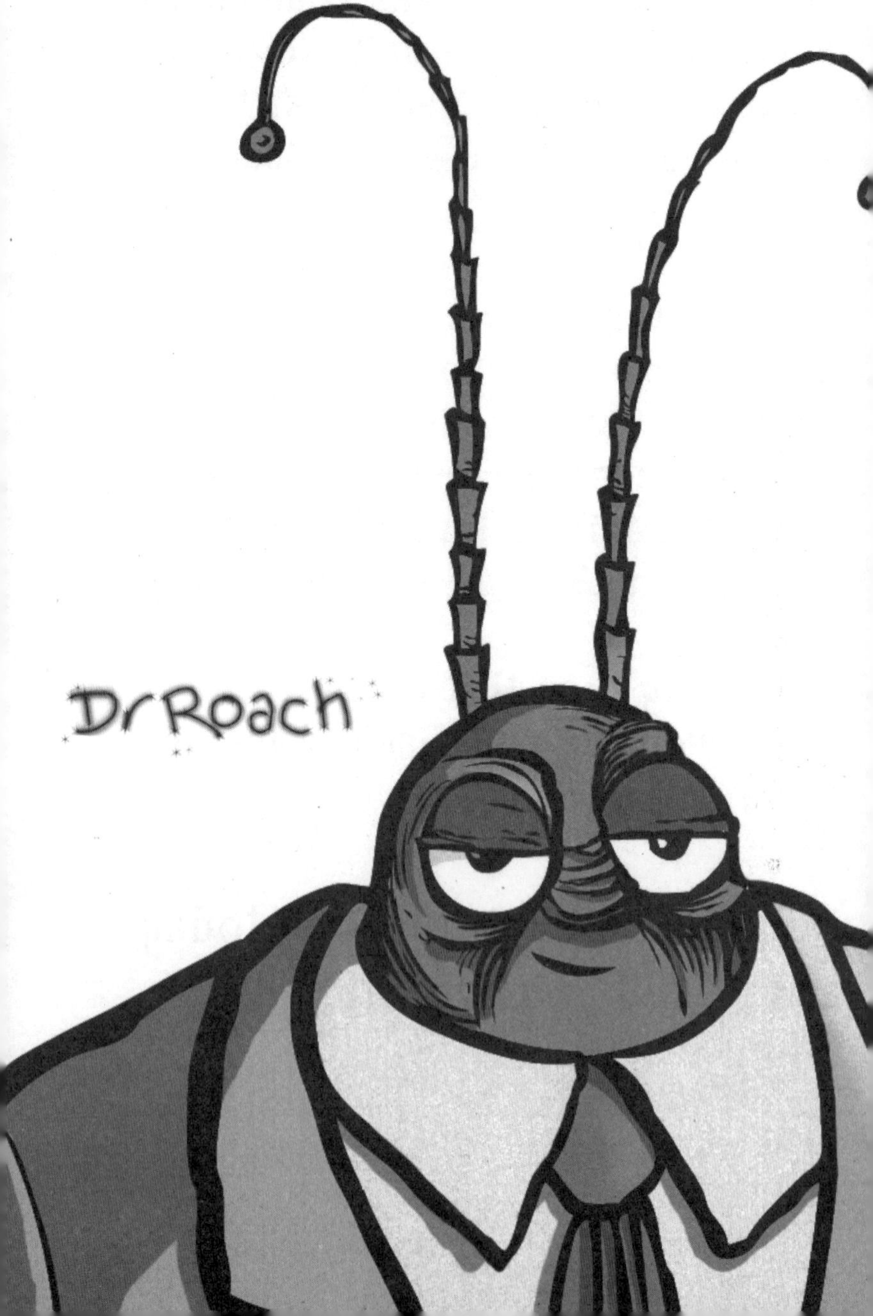